HAMSTER
HEROES

BY PETER BENTLY
& JOHN BOND

HarperCollins *Children's Books*

HAMSTERS look cute when they're cosy and curled.

They like a nice snooze after **SAVING THE WORLD.**

HAMSTER HEROES

To Jiffy, Fluff, Pom-Pom and Pushkin,
currently fighting baddies in HamHeaven

P.B.

For Jazz and Kobe

J.B.

First published in the United Kingdom by HarperCollins *Children's Books* in 2023

HarperCollins *Children's Books* is a division of HarperCollins*Publishers* Ltd
1 London Bridge Street, London SE1 9GF

www.harpercollins.co.uk

HarperCollins*Publishers*
Macken House, 39/40 Mayor Street Upper, Dublin 1, D01 C9W8, Ireland

1 3 5 7 9 10 8 6 4 2

Text copyright © Peter Bently 2023
Illustrations copyright © John Bond 2023

ISBN: 978-0-00-846925-2

Printed in the United Kingdom

They're nibbling their lunch when the message comes through:

"HAMSTERS ASSEMBLE AT HERO HQ!"

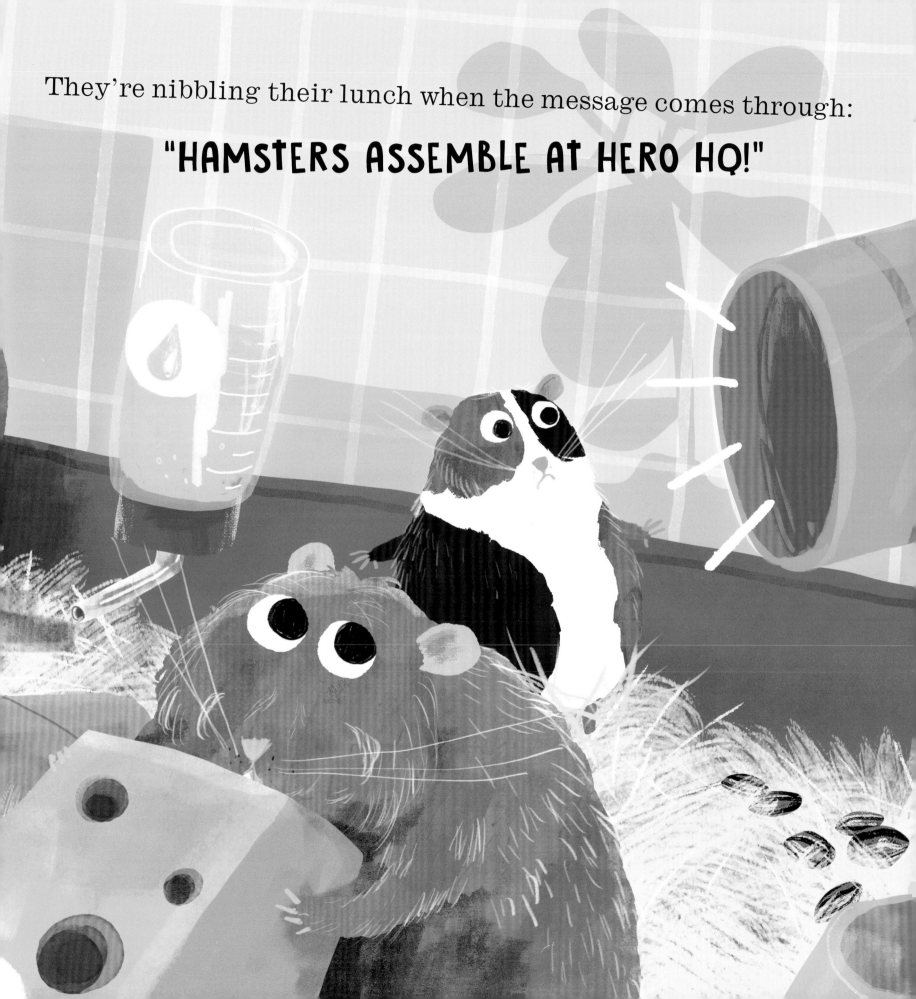

They creep from their cages when nobody sees

(they sometimes leave dummies they've carved out of cheese. . .)

And scurry down long secret tunnels, unseen,
then zoom to HQ in their HamSubmarine.

There's no time to lose when they get to their base.
There are **ALIEN GERBILS** invading from space!

"No problem!" says Pom-Pom. "I'll soon make them scram!"
With a **WHOOSH!** she transforms! She becomes –

HAMMERHAM!

With a **WHACK!** and a **WHAM!** and a grin on her face,
she wallops those aliens back into space!

The hamsters all cheer. But they can't relax yet . . . there's news from HQ of **another** big threat!

The city's in danger! Prepare for a thriller!
Who'll stop **CHINZILLA**, the **GIANT** CHINCHILLA?

Jiffy steps forward. "Just leave this to me!"
WHOOSH! He's transforming as quick as can be . . .

Is it an eagle, or is it a plane? No! It's

SUPERHAM off to the rescue again!

He soars through the sky, the most splendid of sights,
with his bright-orange swimming trunks over his tights!

The monster is in for a nasty surprise
as **SUPERHAM** turns on his laser-beam eyes . . .

"OUCH!" In a moment that big monster hotshot runs away squealing and clutching his hot bot!

Pushkin says, "Yay! Now it's snack time. Let's eat! Let's bust out the broccoli, just for a treat."

Then **CRACKLE!** and **WHIRR!** goes the screen at HQ – and the heroes' **WORST ENEMY** comes into view!

"It's **GOLDENPAW GUINEA-PIG!**" everyone gasps,
as over the giant screen Goldenpaw rasps.

"Mwah-hah-hah! With my genius **VEG-E-TRON** ray,
I will steal the world's broccoli! **HAVE A NICE DAY!**"

Pushkin is in for a nasty surprise
as the broccoli **vanishes** under her eyes!

"NOOOO!" hollers Pushkin. She's in a right sulk.
Uh-oh! Watch out! She's becoming . . .

She leads all the heroes to Goldenpaw's lair.
CRASH! go the gates – but the baddie's not there!

MWAH HAH HA

The Bulk bellows, "There he is, trying to flee!"
"Mwah-hah!" cries the villain. "You'll never catch **ME!**"

He jumps in his jet in a scampering dash –
but Hammerham's hammer soon stops him! **KER-SMASH!**

But the baddie ejects in a jet-propelled pack
with a big stash of broccoli strapped to his back!

Goldenpaw's in for a bit of a shock when Fluff becomes

SPIDERHAM

ready to rock!

"Just wait!" cries the hero. "We're not finished yet!"
And the villain flies right into Spiderham's net!

"Rats! Foiled again!" they hear Goldenpaw wail,
as the hamster police take him straight off to jail.

The heroes all cheer as he's taken away.

"We saved the world's broccoli!
HIP HIP HOORAY!"

So next time your hamsters are curled in their nest,
they're probably having a well-deserved rest.

Till the order comes through that makes all baddies tremble:
"The world is in danger . . .

...HAMSTERS ASSEMBLE!"